Tobin's Spirit Guide

Tobin's Spirit Guide

OFFICIAL **GHOSTBUSTERS**™ EDITION

WRITTEN BY

Dr. Ray Stantz, Dr. Egon Spengler, and Erik Burnham

ILLUSTRATED BY

Kyle Hotz

INSIGHT EDITIONS

San Rafael, California

Greetings!

It became apparent to me some years ago that the average citizen simply does not have the tools at hand to easily identify any paranormal entity that may be manifesting in their vicinity at a given time.

Considering that such phenomena are on the rise in our world, I'm sure you can understand my concern; knowledge is a powerful asset and can make all the difference in surviving a paranormal encounter unscathed.

For help in this regard, my fellow Ghostbusters and I have most often turned to the seminal work of John Tobin, whose eponymous spirit guide has provided us with a wealth of insight into the realm of the supernatural. However, the unabridged edition weighs in at somewhere around 35 pounds, which makes it very comprehensive but not convenient as a go-to reference for John and Jane Q. Public.

And that's how inspiration struck.

I asked myself, what if we compiled and adapted some of the more relevant sections from *Tobin's Spirit Guide*, with the addition of modern insight from our own recent cases? We could disseminate some helpful information in layman's terms without breaking anyone's back in the process.

My colleague Dr. Egon Spengler and I put in weeks of effort to boil the essence of *Tobin's* down into this slim pocket reference you now hold in your hands: a book that contains basic information on some of the most common types of entities that manifest themselves on this side of the dimensional wall, be they spirit, demon, or even minor gods with aspirations to end life as we know it via destruction, subjugation, or both.

For our New York City readers, we have compiled a brief list of some of the more frustratingly recurrent local ghosts, as well as their preferred haunting grounds.

Finally, for the curious, this book also contains information on some of our high-profile busts, entities that we hope never show their metaphorical faces on this plane of existence again—but if they do, you'll know what to look for.

And then, of course, you'll know who to call.

It should go without saying that should you become aware of any spirit, specter, ghost, demon, poltergeist, will-o'-the-wisp, revenant, shade, wraith, apparition, spook, or a heavy presence of any kind, you should first remove yourself from the area before attempting to classify or make sense of said phenomenon.

In the meantime, I congratulate you on taking this first step toward greater knowledge of what lies beyond.

See you on the other side!

—Dr. Ray Stantz
New York, NY

Section I: Ghosts of New York

A FEW FEARSOME PHANTOMS FOUND IN THE FIVE BOROUGHS

New York City is known as the "city that never sleeps," but with one of the highest natural concentrations of ghosts in the known world, it might as well be called the "city that never rests in peace."

From the public library to the Foley Square courthouse; from Madison Avenue to Central Park; the New York metropolitan area is full of iconic locations plagued by supernatural phenomena.

This section contains information on some of the high-profile manifestations we've discovered anchored in and around the Big Apple.

The New York Subway Specters

VARIABLE CLASS; MOST OFTEN I OR III. ANCHORED TO NYC SUBWAY TUNNELS, TRAINS, AND STATIONS.

The New York subway system boasts an impressive number of ghosts—the apparitions of accident victims, the murdered, and, of course, suicides populate the tunnels, stations, and trains of the metropolitan subway lines. Usually these spirits anchor themselves to one spot and remain invisible; this spot won't necessarily be the location where they died, but it will be one in which they feel relatively at peace.

Of course, this is New York, so "at peace" is a relative term. With a constant wave of commuters, the ghosts' calm is continuously under assault. The least aggressive of these spirits will try to ward off the living by creating minor electrical disruptions (flickering lights or rapid battery loss in any personal electronic devices) or by emanating a persistent creepy vibe until the unwanted commuter moves on.

When a ghost's patience finally reaches breaking point, it may become visible and throw what can best be described as—if you'll excuse a momentary descent into the vernacular—the mother of all hissy fits.

Because many of these exasperated apparitions were created by grisly, train-impact-related incidents, their frequent manifestations have led to a sharp increase in pedestrian traffic on the streets of New York, especially among tourists.

Pappy Sargassi

CLASS IV. NONCORPOREAL. MANIFESTS AT VARIOUS NYC LOCATIONS OF THE SARGASSI'S SEAFOOD RESTAURANT CHAIN.

Enzo "Pappy" Sargassi, founder of the successful seafood restaurant Sargassi's, was lost at sea on a fishing trip in 1954.

Sargassi's ghost began to manifest at different branches of Sargassi's restaurants in the late 1970s, including the Brooklyn, Staten Island, and Times Square outlets, before finding a permanent home in the dining room of the branch located in the Sedgewick Hotel lobby.

In and of itself, the Sargassi ghost wasn't particularly bothersome, but it didn't manifest alone; it was accompanied by a class IV spectral shark that would chase Sargassi around the restaurant until it captured and devoured him. (Not a particularly appetizing sight for restaurant patrons.)

Called in to deal with Pappy, we trapped the more aggressive entity, the shark, first; as soon as it was gone, Sargassi's ghost faded away on its own. To date, it has not manifested again.

The Driver

CLASS III. CORPOREAL ONLY WHEN IT MANIFESTS IN THE CONFINES OF A TAXICAB. LOCATION: MADISON AVENUE

The "Driver" is an entity that randomly manifests in taxicabs, taking control of the vehicle and embarking on a wild, and potentially dangerous, joyride.

While this ghost consistently manifests in the same general location—Madison Avenue—and always in a taxicab, it has proven difficult to identify the origins of the spirit. One theory suggests that the entity was originally a driver for the precursor to New York's modern taxi service—a fleet of electric hansoms that began taking passengers in 1897. Another theory posits that the Driver could be the result of a fatal incident where a taxicab drove into the Harlem River in the 1950s.

Of course, this is all speculation that assumes the ghost's predilection for taking control of a cab is proof of its occupation prior to death. We should also consider that the person from whom the spirit is derived might have died as a taxicab passenger or simply had a strong desire to drive that carried through to the afterlife. Whatever the true nature of the ghost, its random manifestations have made it extremely difficult to predict its movements, and thus trap. (Given how hard it can be to catch a cab in this city, catching a specific one is borderline impossible.)

Those who have encountered this entity describe it as a stereotypically ghoulish zombie with rotting flesh, ragged clothes, and a stench worse than a garbage scow on a summer day.

The Green Ghost (aka "Slimer")

CLASS V. FULL-ROAMING VAPOR. FORMERLY ANCHORED TO THE TWELFTH FLOOR OF THE SEDGEWICK HOTEL.

This spirit, which had been haunting the twelfth floor of the Sedgewick Hotel on Park Avenue since the mid-1920s, became the subject of the first full field test of the Ghostbusters' proprietary equipment. During the encounter, a messy collision with our colleague Dr. Venkman led us to nickname the ghost "Slimer."

Our best guess at the ghost's origins dates back to the apocalyptic Cult of Gozer, which held meetings at the Sedgewick in the early 1920s, finally wearing out its welcome when an animal sacrifice went awry. According to our research, it's most likely that the cult's rituals conjured a "hungry spirit"—a ghost that can never sate its inhuman appetite—as a destructive punishment for the world.

During our encounter with Slimer, we noticed the lingering aftereffects of its presence: the persistent stench of rancid meat and an increase in the heaviness of the air similar to stifling humidity. There were also piles of chewed food and overturned furniture and an unusual amount of exuded ectoplasm.

The ghost is mostly nocturnal, has a rudimentary intelligence, and exhibits low levels of telekinetic ability. That said, it isn't a stereotypical poltergeist (for more on poltergeists, see the entry on page 31); its behavior tends more toward gluttony, not rage.

And it is a glutton! Since whatever it consumes immediately passes through its body and onto the floor, it can never be sated.

Although we initially trapped Slimer at the Sedgewick Hotel, it was released from captivity when our original containment unit was shut down by Walter Peck, then of the Environmental Protection Agency. Once we recaptured the ghost, we placed it in a smaller containment unit—an ionized glass cage that allowed us to study its properties and behavior directly.

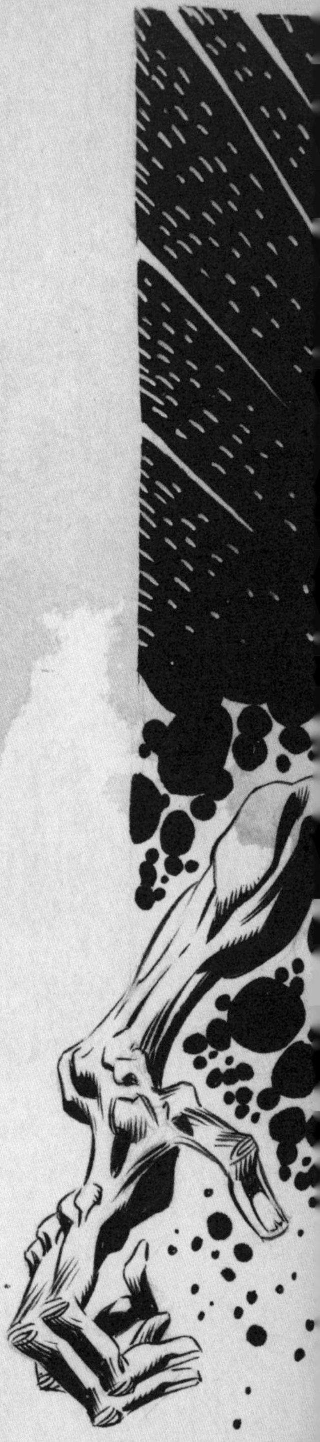

The Spider Witch

CLASS VI. CORPOREAL. ANCHORED TO THE TWELFTH FLOOR OF THE SEDGEWICK HOTEL.

The Sedgewick Hotel, in which we trapped Slimer, was also host to a far more malevolent presence known as the Spider Witch. From diaries recovered at the scene of the haunting, we were able to piece together the following:

A hotel resident in the 1920s, Evelyn Lewis, was a member of Ivo Shandor's Gozerian Cult (see section V for more information), which often hosted meetings in her suite. Unlike the other members of the cult, she had ambitions beyond bringing about the end of the physical world; she wanted to be powerful in the afterlife and was a regular practitioner of human sacrifice in order to achieve that end.

Her body, the result of an apparent suicide, was found in her suite amid a pile of destroyed furniture that had been arranged into a nest-like structure. Around the

"nest" were neatly stacked piles of human remains. Blood stained the carpets and also the walls, where it was used to write the woman's last words: "I am not done."

Hotel staff sealed off the room, but years later remodeling work on the Sedgewick uncovered the suite and woke the spirit of Evelyn Lewis, which manifested as a large, corporeal, human/spider hybrid. (It was the spitting image of a Japanese *jorōgumo*! You just don't see those kinds of ghosts in the States.)

The Spider Witch's atomic cohesion made it as solid as flesh and blood; the ghost wasn't able to easily leave the suite and was in the process of ripping a hole in the wall when we arrived to deal with the matter. It took four of us at least an hour—and three proton grenades—to bring her down. The spirits of her five most recent victims appeared and thanked us before fading away, presumably to join the other ghostly residents of the hotel.

The Librarian (aka The Gray Lady)

CLASS IV. ANCHORED TO THE NEW YORK PUBLIC LIBRARY.

In 1924, Eleanor Twitty, the head librarian of the New York Public Library, vanished. She was last seen at the library itself, and policemen who searched the entire building found no trace of her. A search of her apartment turned up the same results. She was gone.

But in 1925, patrons and other librarians started to notice signs of her presence; her favorite books began to appear regularly on the front desk in the morning, and people who spoke above a whisper would be shushed from the shadows. Patrons using the reference section also reported feeling that they were being watched by Twitty.

The ghost appeared frequently in this manner until 1929, then went dormant. The Librarian—also known as the Gray Lady—manifested again many years later, appearing openly in the lower levels of the library, actively harassing both patrons and staff and leaving a plentiful amount of ectoplasmic discharge in her wake.

The Gray Lady was the first spirit that the founding members of the Ghostbusters faced together—as this was our first direct supernatural encounter, we were admittedly not as prepared as we should have been.

We ultimately decided to rush the ghost, which seemed like a good idea at the time. Our hypothesis was that when approached with no signs of fear, the ghost would disperse. Instead, it metamorphosed into a more terrifying form and let out a blood-curdling scream. Lacking any offensive capabilities, we opted for a strategic retreat. It wasn't a total wash, however. The data we collected was invaluable in the design and calibration of our proprietary ghost-trapping equipment.

We returned to the library more than once in the following months to seek out and trap the Gray Lady, but she remained out of reach. Eventually, we were led to secret catacombs beneath the library, where Eleanor Twitty's corpse was discovered. The Librarian attacked us again there, in her aggressive, bestial form, but this time she was no match for us—or rather, our proton streams.

The Scoleri Brothers

CLASS IV. NONCORPOREAL ELEMENTAL SPIRITS.
ANCHORED TO THE FOLEY SQUARE COURTHOUSE.

Several types of ghosts may be witnessed at courthouses, but most common are the victims of murderers facing trial. These spirits tend not to be troublesome—they are ready to pass on but are determined to first witness justice done in their name.

Also prevalent are the ghosts of judges and attorneys who cannot help but be drawn to the more salacious and newsworthy cases. If they are particularly potent spirits, they may try to influence the proceedings—from whispering legal advice into a lawyer's ear to terrorizing a defendant they know to be guilty.

The final type are the ghosts of the guilty. Some of these grow penitent and pass on; the rest seethe with indignation and do their best to disrupt the legal proceedings.

Charged with murder, Nunzio and Tony Scoleri were sentenced to death by electric chair on the order of Judge Stephen Wexler, then new to the bench. Many years later, the Ghostbusters found themselves in the courtroom of the then veteran Judge Wexler on a public nuisance charge (the use of public utility access to investigate a river of psychomagnotheric ectoplasm).

When Wexler became extremely agitated with us in the presence of the slime we had collected, his negativity reacted with the properties of the ectoplasm, allowing the Scoleris to manifest and wreak havoc.

The Scoleris appeared to be attached to the electric chairs they were executed in and were able to take full elemental control of electricity, which they used to attempt to revenge themselves upon the judge.

The charges against us were dropped, and we were allowed to use our equipment to swiftly capture the Scoleris. The most notable aspect of the incident was the powerful manner in which the slime reacted to Wexler. Despite our request to collect further data, his honor declined our offer of a full physical workup.

Ellen Gold

CLASS IV. SEMICORPOREAL. ANCHORED TO THE NOW DESTROYED WANDER HILLS ORPHANAGE IN THE BOROUGH OF QUEENS.

A member of a prominent New York family, Ellen Gold had inherited mental instability from her mother's side of the family, a condition kept hidden to maintain the Golds' reputation in society.

To keep Ellen both out of sight and out of mind, the Golds arranged to have her installed as the headmistress of the Wander Hills Orphanage in Queens. Ellen ran the orphanage ably, but her instability often led her to punish the children for "naughtiness" even when they were well behaved. One former employee was quoted as saying that Ellen would "lock the children in their rooms at the drop of a hat and wouldn't release them before dawn for any reason."

In 1920, under one such lockdown, tragedy struck when a lightning storm set fire to the orphanage in the middle of the night. Even as the orphanage burned to the ground, Ellen wouldn't let the children leave, and both she and her pupils died in the blaze.

Over time, the incident was forgotten—although people living in homes built over the site of the razed orphanage reported that they could often hear children crying during rainstorms.

Eventually, the phantom orphans began to materialize at regular intervals. However, it wasn't until psychokinetic energy was at an all-time high during the arrival of the deity Gozer (see section V) that it became easier for ghosts to cross over to this plane of existence, and Ellen Gold herself finally manifested.

The spirit incarnation of Gold was aggressive and prone to paranoid ranting, which matched accounts of her behavior when alive. The entity frustrated our initial attempts at proton restraint by throwing the ghosts of the orphans into our line of fire. When we were finally able to circle around behind her, it was a simple matter to zap her and trap her.

Dream Ghost

CLASS IV. NONCORPOREAL. ANCHORED TO FORT DETMERRING. MANIFESTS ONLY WHEN A SLEEPING INDIVIDUAL IS PRESENT.

Dream ghosts are benign entities that can only fully manifest on this plane of existence while in the presence of a sleeping individual. They should not be confused with those entities that enter the subconscious mind of a sleeping individual, usually to do harm (for more on nocturnal entities, see the entry on the Sandman on page 41).

New York's own Fort Detmerring is host to such an entity, rumored to be the sweetheart of an officer who was posted at the fort back when it was a fully functioning military stronghold.

The rooms the spirit frequents—the officer's quarters, in particular—are identifiable by a palpable feeling of exhaustion; crossing the threshold into one of these rooms can leave you feeling as though you haven't slept for days. Leaving the room can immediately reverse the effect.

After extensive research into the matter, we were able to conclude that the Detmerring entity was of no danger to the general public. Dr. Stantz nevertheless continues to monitor the site regularly.

The Phantom Jogger

CLASS III. CORPOREAL BUT SEMI-TRANSPARENT. ANCHORED TO CENTRAL PARK. MANIFESTS ON THE PARK'S MANY RUNNING PATHS.

Each time it manifested, the Phantom Jogger could actually be seen checking its pulse as though it still had a beating heart. It's most likely that the Jogger wasn't aware that it had actually passed on, which isn't uncommon in the case of an instantaneous death—a sudden heart attack could have killed the Jogger before he had the chance to register his own passing (for more on this type of entity, see the entry on confused spirits on page 34).

The Jogger manifested several times each day, and although its sudden appearance would spook other runners and occasionally the horses on the bridle paths, it was mostly benign. However, the more it appeared, the more aggressive it became, until it resorted to shoving others out of its path.

The ghost's predictable route made it relatively easy to capture; we simply calculated the time of its next manifestation and stationed Dr. Venkman at a park bench near the reservoir with a ghost trap.

Section II: Assorted Apparitions

A MÉLANGE OF THE MACABRE

There are a great many ghosts out there with names, identities, and specific motivations, but it's not always the case that ghosts have such well-defined characteristics.

Sometimes a spirit is merely the embodiment of a specific memory or emotion, or a victim of circumstance that can't build up the momentum or desire to move on to the next plane of existence. These are the kind of ghosts you're most likely to run across in the field and the kind that make up a good chunk of our caseload.

This section will identify some of the more common entities that you may come into contact with.

Be vigilant!

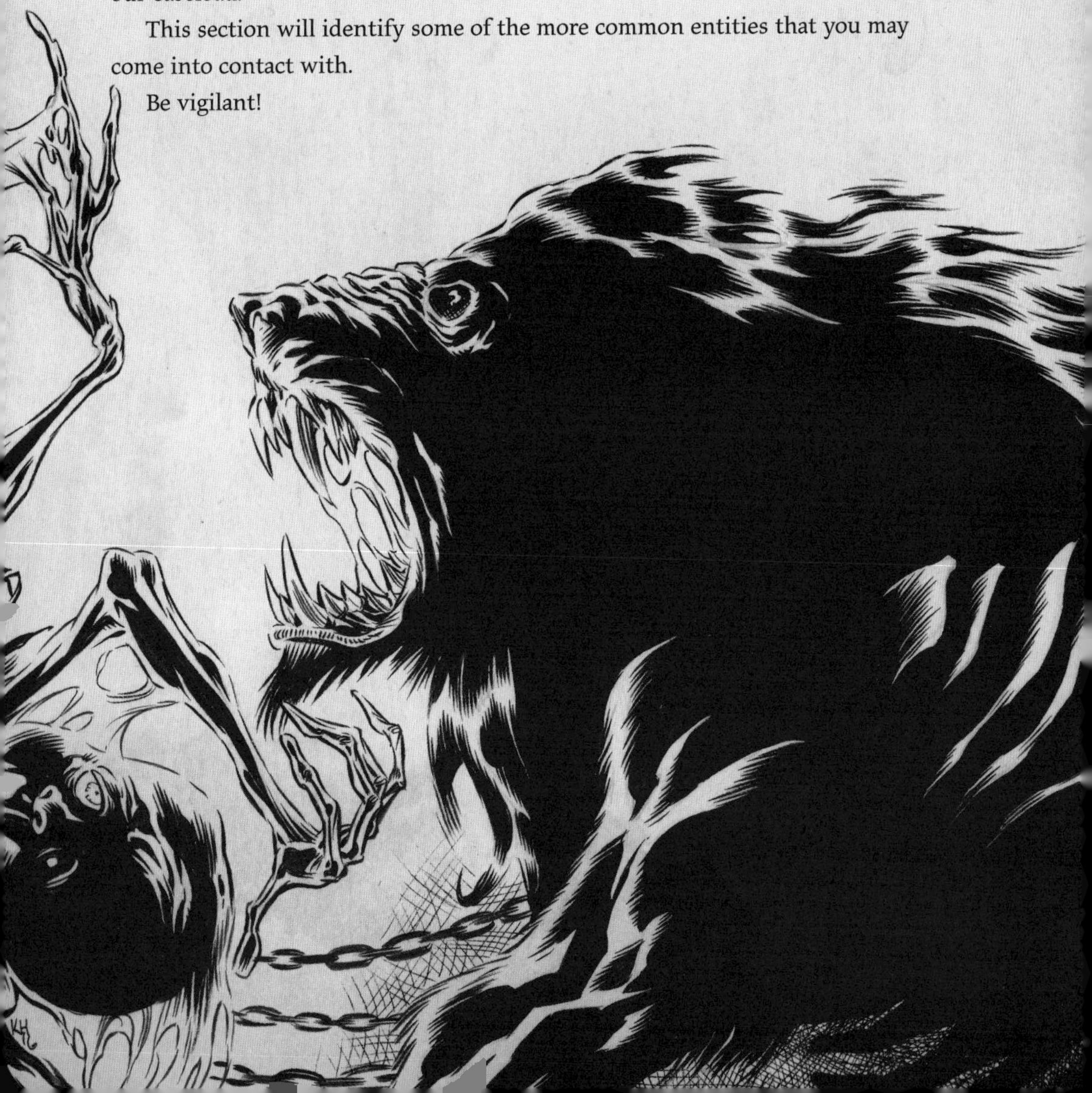

Spectrally Animated Clothing

CLASS II. NONCORPOREAL BUT ABLE TO TAKE POSSESSION OF APPAREL.

Sometimes spirits that desire a body of their own but are unable to take possession of a sentient being will inhabit the next best thing: items of clothing. Possessed garments can often be identified by rips or stains that appear at random or by a sudden change of location; clothes left folded in a dresser may appear the next day hanging in a closet, for example.

Typically such an inhabitation is, at worst, an inconvenience. The spirit is often content to be a passenger and will eventually move on of its own accord. That said, there is a remote chance that this incomplete spirit will evolve and begin to crave more of a presence in the physical world. Lacking any higher logic, the entity may attempt to drive away or harm a living human in an attempt to usurp their place. Such was the case of Sebastian Whitlow, who was found strangled to death near Hoboken, New Jersey, in 1897. The sleeves of his overcoat were wrapped around his neck, and he was gripping its lapels as though, the police noted, he were "locked in a life-or-death struggle." Sebastian Whitlow's case remains an outlier, but one worth noting.

If you see signs that an article of your clothing may be possessed, the best strategy is to burn it—simply throwing out the garment or donating it is not a solution. Once the preferred item has been properly destroyed, the possessing spirit should move on.

Crybaby Ghosts

CLASS III OR VI.
NONCORPOREAL. TYPICALLY
ANCHORED TO RURAL BRIDGES.

A "crybaby" manifestation stems from the drowning of a child within close proximity to a bridge. (Specifically, a rural bridge—we find that urban areas boast a higher success rate in accident rescue.) At this time it remains a mystery why bridges in particular anchor crybaby spirits to this plane of existence, but the phenomenon has been consistent—especially in the state of Ohio, home to the largest collection of crybaby bridges in the United States and, possibly, the world.

Typically, these apparitions mean no *direct* harm, but their sudden appearances have been known to cause extreme distress and subsequent accidents, and depending on traffic and elevation, this can spell disaster.

Even when they do not visually manifest, crybaby spirits will make their presence known to any passersby—especially at night—by letting out chilling cries that echo from the underside of the bridge they are bound to.

Panic and trauma define this particular type of spirit, and whenever possible, it's preferable to help them move on. In essence, they're the echoes of frightened children—meeting them with fear will exacerbate the situation, but patience and a soothing tone can calm them and enable them to peacefully disperse.

Animal Spirits

CLASS VI. MAY BE CORPOREAL. TEND TO DISPLAY THE SAME TRAITS AS LIVING SPECIMENS, ALBEIT HIGHLY AMPLIFIED.

Most people assume that a haunting carried out by an animal's spirit is of less concern than a haunting perpetrated by the spirit of a human being. That would be a mistake. Animal ghosts have a remarkable consistency, displaying many of the same behaviors that they did in life: They'll attempt to stake their claim on territory, assert dominance, and, in the case of predators, actively stalk prey.

These corporeal drives and instincts are not only present, but are typically amplified in spirits, generally resulting in aggression—especially toward the living. The most consistent exceptions to this are the ghosts of pet dogs, who maintain a loyalty to those they knew in life. Pet cats, however, retain their earthly aloofness.

The last decade has seen a sharp rise in animal-related hauntings in the Midwestern region of the United States, with an unusual concentration in Chicago. Indeed, the Windy City has seen the ghosts of slaughtered cattle stampeding through the streets and goring pedestrians on the Magnificent Mile; an attempted invasion of Lake Michigan by a massive spectral shark from Shedd Aquarium; and even the reanimation of the infamous man-eating lions known as the Ghost and the Darkness displayed at Chicago's Field Museum of Natural History. Investigations into why Chicago seems to be a hotbed for this type of haunting are ongoing.

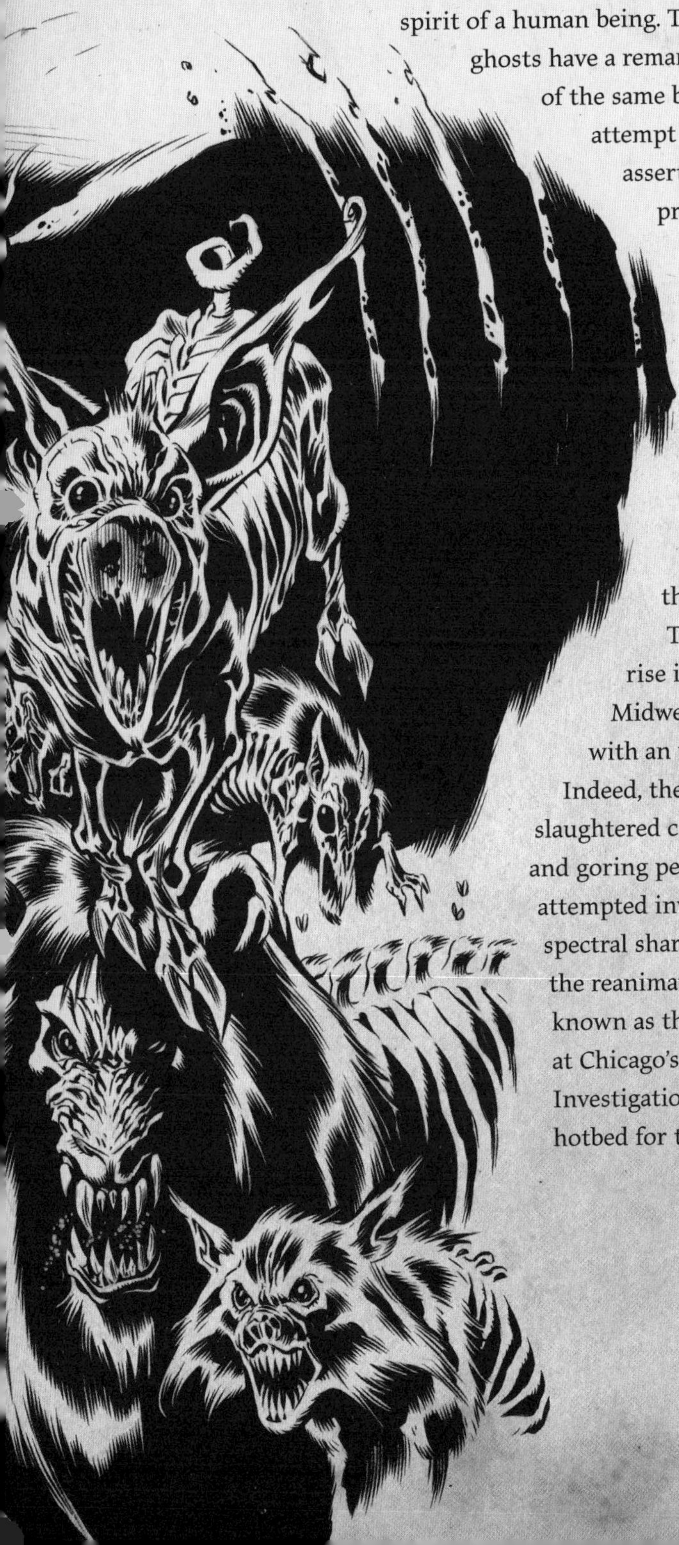

Spirit Guide

CLASS III. DOES NOT MANIFEST IN THE PHYSICAL WORLD.

This particular phenomenon has been a difficult one to research. By its very nature, a spirit guide is not easily observed and is believed to appear only in dreams.

One might consider the phenomenon a mass delusion, but unconnected reports of these entities have popped up around the world, with a great deal of consistency in the details of the descriptions. The spirit is a comforting presence that visits during deep sleep. It wears dark clothes and its eyes are almost always hidden from view (covered by a cloak, sunglasses, or even a blindfold). The guide warns the dreamer of future troubles and gives counsel in how to prepare for them.

To each dreamer, the presence is familiar yet unrecognizable; the religious believe it to be a holy vision. Atheists have come to consider it proof of a shared human subconscious.

We've had the opportunity to study the brainwaves of one individual contacted by a spirit guide: Dr. Ray Stantz, the coauthor of this book. The subject's electroencephalogram revealed abnormal activity; delta and gamma wave frequencies were both present over the course of several readings.

That said, at this time, we do not believe contact with these beings is dangerous.

Poltergeists

CLASS II, III, OR V. NONCORPOREAL. TELEKINETIC.

Poltergeists—or "noisy ghosts"—are known to levitate objects telekinetically, moan at all hours of the night, and endlessly shake phantom chains. When you hear about "things that go bump in the night," that's a poltergeist.

One trait unique to poltergeists is their tendency to focus attention on the torment of individuals, as opposed to haunting specific locations—they have even been known to haunt entire family lines. (Poltergeists are able to immediately identify the descendants of anyone they have previously taken a dislike to.)

Poltergeists are made manifest by a powerful emotion—be it love, sadness, or anger—but no matter which emotion forms their core, it eventually evolves into blind, violent rage. The only option the average citizen has when targeted by a poltergeist is to call in the Ghostbusters! Should that not be an option, one's safest bet is to vacate that poltergeist's territory; the ghost will at that point become less aggressive, maybe even dormant.

Elemental Spirits

CLASS III OR V. GENERALLY NONCORPOREAL. PSYCHOKINETIC USE OF ONE OF THE FOUR MAIN ELEMENTS.

Like the poltergeist, an elemental spirit is made manifest by powerful emotion and can directly affect its environs by way of telekinesis.

Unlike the poltergeist, an elemental spirit (as its designation would suggest) is connected to one of the four primal elements—fire (including electricity), air, water (including ice), or earth—and it will manipulate that element exclusively. The elemental spirit is also far less likely to concern itself with a vendetta against a particular individual or restrict itself to a single location; instead it will manifest across a larger geographical area. It's not unheard of for these entities to haunt an entire county, as with the headless horseman of Westchester County, New York, made famous for its appearances near the village of Sleepy Hollow.

Over the course of several cases, we've discovered another major difference between the typical poltergeist and elemental spirits: While poltergeists are untethered to any sort of mortal identity, elemental spirits often retain aspects of any humanity they once had, and this can be instrumental in the resolution of a haunting.

We speculate that much of the rage exhibited by elemental spirits springs from an inability to grasp the full memory of their identity. They tend to disperse peacefully as soon as they are able to remember their past life, such as the case of the elemental spirit of Francis Harding, a teenager lost in the sinking of the *John Milton,* a ship captained by his father, in 1858. The Ghostbusters were able to assist the spirit in finding the grave of his father, allowing the late Francis to finally be at peace.

Confused Spirits

CLASS IV. TYPICALLY CORPOREAL.

A confused spirit is a ghost that has yet to process the fact that it has passed on. It believes itself to be fully alive and is often completely aware of its identity, although it may remain in denial indefinitely about its ghostly state.

The deaths of those who come back as confused spirits were typically both unexpected and instantaneous. Whether these deaths were caused by accident, natural causes, or murder makes little difference; the event is sudden enough that the mind (and, by extension, the soul) can't properly register the transition.

As in most hauntings, the confused spirit often has some kind of unfinished business to attend to, but its befuddlement makes the task difficult, and it will often fall into repetitive patterns, like a traveler passing across the same stretch of road, day after day.

Typically benign, these spirits appear to be human—they're even fully corporeal and completely oblivious to their condition. (Or, rather, their atomic cohesion is stable enough to mimic the physical substance of a living being.). However, their behavior may become unpredictable if they are made aware of their status; some may peacefully disperse, while others grow violent.

As always, if these ghosts are doing no harm, it's best to let them be. If they insist on interaction, feel free to make small talk. It's not uncommon to encounter confused spirits in and around roads and highways. If they ask for a ride, use your best judgment. Remember, ectoplasm can badly stain upholstery.

Household Spirits

CLASS III. CORPOREAL.

Common in European communities, household spirits—such as the Russian *domoviye*, Scottish brownie, or German *kobold*—were eventually brought to North America by immigrants, albeit in limited numbers.

These spirits are invisible but generally corporeal enough to affect their environment. Once they have accepted an invitation to join a human household, they tend to assume multiple duties—anything from common domestic chores to warding off evil spirits and providing their hosts with premonitions of the future.

Domoviye in particular have a demonstrative manner of hinting at forthcoming events: Laughter signals good times; sobbing signals misfortune; strumming a comb predicts a wedding, and becoming fully visible to the host family foretells a death.

In return for their service, they demand respect and also forgiveness on the rare occasion that they cause a little mischief to blow off steam. (Such mischief may include breaking plates, consuming desserts or beer, and, in the case of the *domoviye*, roughly pinching their human hosts while they sleep.)

If you offend a household spirit, there are rituals that can be undertaken that will smooth over (almost) any rift. The most common involves a loud apology, tossing salt over one's left shoulder, and leaving out a gift of tobacco or beer. But sometimes, no apology is enough. The offended spirit will then either abandon a host's house or grow more and more aggressive until the host is driven out—alive or otherwise.

Phantom Vehicles

CLASS V. CAN BE BOTH CORPOREAL AND NONCORPOREAL.
OFTEN ANCHORED TO A ROUTE STRETCHING ANYWHERE FROM
A FEW HUNDRED FEET TO THOUSANDS OF MILES.

There are several distinct types of phantom vehicles. Some manifest as a result of being exposed to an emotionally charged event. For example, the funeral train that returned the body of Abraham Lincoln to his hometown of Springfield, Illinois, can be seen in phantom form, making its way westward from Washington, DC, once each year. This apparition comes complete with a full complement of Union soldiers and a coffin draped in the American flag. It never quite manages to complete the trip before sunrise.

Ships lost at sea (for example, the famed *Flying Dutchman*) are known to haunt open ocean waters and bring death (or at least misfortune) to any who should chance to see them.

A far more sinister manifestation comes in the form of possessed vehicles that lie in wait for unsuspecting passengers. These vehicles—ships, coaches, trains, and automobiles—are manned by unseen operators that attempt to lure hasty victims aboard. Those lucky few who have encountered these apparitions but opted not to embark have reported an indescribable sense of dread surrounding the vehicle. Those who choose to accept passage are not seen again.

Possessed Objects

CLASS V. CORPOREAL.

As previously discussed in the entry on spectrally animated clothing (see page 26), some spirits take possession of inanimate objects to gain a corporeal presence.

Instead of simply inhabiting the object, as is the case with possessed garments, spirits that inhabit weightier objects (furniture, appliances, and artwork) will transmogrify their inanimate host, anthropomorphizing it with recognizably organic elements such as eyes, a tongue, and even hands. Objects fastened into place (toilets, for example) will generally remain stationary; other objects might literally grow legs and move about.

Electrical appliances can occasionally be exorcised by severing their connection to a power supply. Destruction of the object will also serve to remove the spirit from its new body.

Section III: Metaspecters

MINOR DEMONS, POWERFUL GHOSTS, AND OTHER NOTABLE ENTITIES

The entities in this section aren't at the level of gods like Gozer, who have the power to end the world. Nevertheless, they are powerful, determined, and quite dangerous. In fact, they account for some of the most difficult cases the Ghostbusters have tackled.

Metaspecters such as the ones detailed in this section have more personality and cunning than lesser ghosts and are also quite capable of specifically targeting individuals or communities on a whim.

The Sandman

CLASS VII. CAN MANIFEST IN THE PHYSICAL WORLD BUT PREFERS TO APPEAR IN THE SUBCONSCIOUS.

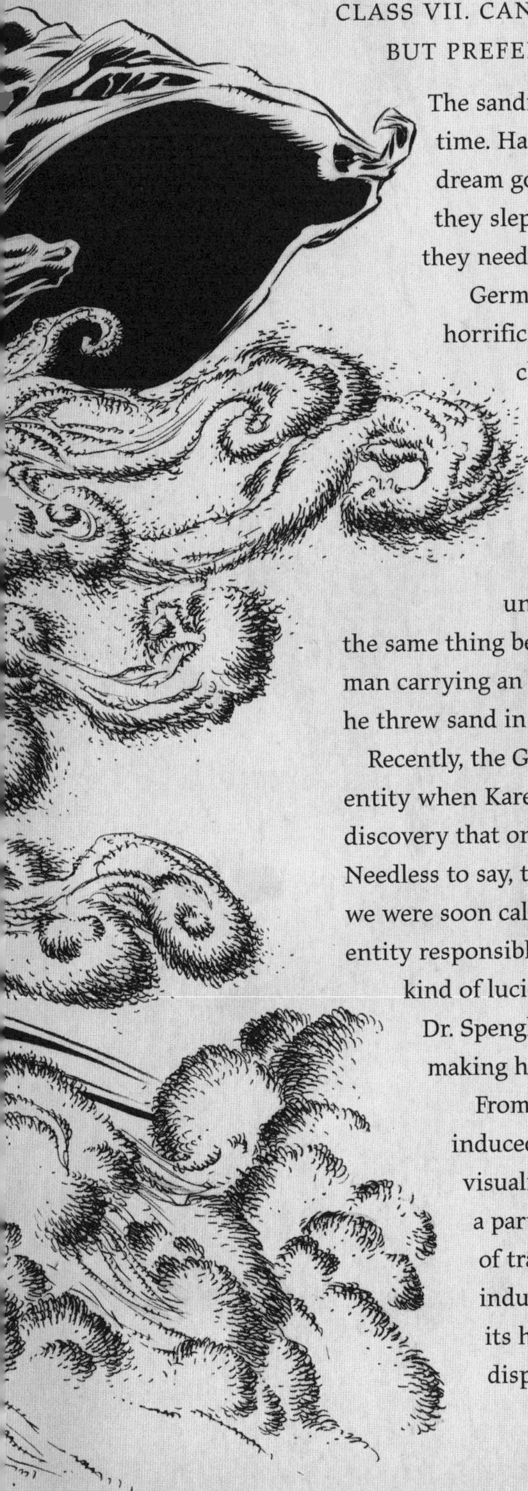

The sandman has been a part of folklore for quite some time. Hans Christian Andersen wrote of Ole Lukøje, a dream god who visited children to tell them stories while they slept and who would dust their eyes with sand if they needed help sleeping.

German author E.T.A. Hoffmann wrote of a more horrific being—a bogeyman type—who punished children who wouldn't sleep by stealing their eyes and feeding them to his own offspring, who lived on the moon.

In 1918, in Avilés, Spain, there were stories of people waking up without their eyes. These people, though blinded, were otherwise unharmed. All the victims remembered dreaming the same thing before awaking with their eyes removed: a cloaked man carrying an hourglass. In the dream, as in Hoffmann's story, he threw sand in their eyes.

Recently, the Ghostbusters came face-to-face with this nocturnal entity when Karen Pearson of Staten Island woke up to the grim discovery that one of her eyes had been removed in her sleep. Needless to say, the local police were baffled by the incident, and we were soon called in to investigate. It didn't take long for the entity responsible to make its presence known, trapping us in a kind of lucid dream state while it focused its attentions on Dr. Spengler, who was suffering from exhaustion at the time, making him an irresistible target.

From within the lucid dream state that the Sandman induced, we were able to attack the entity directly by visualizing our proton equipment and thus making it a part of the dream. Unfortunately, we had no means of trapping the Sandman from inside this psychically induced plane of existence, but we were able to destroy its hourglass totem, which caused the entity to disperse and return us to consciousness.

Ravana

CLASS VII. SEMICORPOREAL (CAN BECOME INTANGIBLE). FREE ROAMING. LIMITED POSSESSOR.

The Rakshasas, a demon race previously thought to exist only in Hindu mythology, are a form of hungry spirit, and the best known of these, Ravana, is the most insatiable of all.

Ravana (and presumably other Rakshasas, to a lesser degree) psychically instills an inhuman hunger in victims that forces them to gorge on food. When these victims put on enough weight for Ravana's liking, they are consumed—sometimes figuratively, with Ravana feeding on the mortal's spirit, and sometimes quite literally, when the human's body is consumed as well. (It is our belief that stories of the Rakshasas are partially responsible for inspiring the witch in the fairy tale "Hansel and Gretel.")

When under the influence of a Rakshasa, a person will eat to the point of physical pain—and continue until they die.

It's difficult to break the connection between one of these entities and the human it is targeting—without the intervention of the Ghostbusters, a victim's only hope is to be sequestered away from all food sources until the Rakshasa loses interest and moves on to find another subject.

When the Ghostbusters faced Ravana, we needed to use high-grade pharmaceutical appetite suppressants just to get close enough to trap it. Once Ravana was trapped, all those already under his psychic influence were freed from their hunger.

Rall

CLASS VII. SEMICORPOREAL. ANCHORED TO A STATUE. INFLUENCES ANIMALS BY WAY OF PARTIAL POSSESSION.

The most reliable accounts state that the demon Rall first manifested in sub-Saharan Africa, roughly three thousand years ago. It is said to have had an affinity for wild beasts, which it regarded as its children. The hunting of these "children" by mankind enraged Rall; it would kill any hunters it came across and leave their corpses for its brood to feed on.

Eventually, the demon was captured and placed in a statue bearing its likeness, which Cleopatra presented to Julius Caesar. Caesar brought it with him when he returned to Rome in 45 BC; in the years since, it has changed hands many times.

Recently, the statue was damaged while in transit to the American Museum of Natural History. When the piece was unveiled to the public, the demon that had been trapped in the sculpture emerged with revenge on its mind.

Rall's presence anthropomorphized the animals of the city—everything from wild pigeons to zoo animals and domestic pets began to speak and act as humans would; they also inherited the demon's hatred of mankind, which resulted in an unheard-of level of rioting and municipal damage.

Rall was a particularly cunning and difficult entity to capture; it was Rall's bestial nature that finally provided the key to its downfall. The Ghostbusters discovered that a tone played at 40 kHz—beyond the range of human hearing but well within Rall's—would incapacitate the demon just long enough for it to be trapped. With Rall contained, the animals of the city immediately returned to normal, with no lingering signs of Rall's influence.

The Collectors

CLASS VI. TRANSDIMENSIONAL.
BOUND BY THE TERMS OF THEIR SUMMONING.

The price for summoning the cadre of demons that have come to be known as the "Collectors" is high. They offer the permanent abduction of whatever target the person who summoned them specifies, but this service comes at the irrevocable cost of one's sanity.

The demons are single-minded and, once engaged, they will pursue their quarry with no thought to secrecy and without being distracted by any other beings they may encounter. This has led to more firsthand accounts of their activities than might be expected, given that the Collectors are such dangerous entities.

The demons tend to take on the appearance of their prey, becoming a supernatural duplicate that brings to mind the German concept of the doppelganger. (These are complementary concepts, and any potential relationship between the two bears further study.)

The Ghostbusters were captured by the Collectors and deposited in some kind of interdimensional limbo. Fortunately, we were able to escape by rewiring a proton pack to explode. Although we'd been trapped for just a few hours, we discovered that months had passed in New York, an interesting note for any future interdimensional research.

Further investigation revealed that the Collectors had been sent after us by Janosz Poha (see entry on Vigo the Carpathian on page 64), who had been possessed by the demon Idulnas. When Idulnas tried to avoid paying the price for summoning the Collectors, hoping they would take Poha's sanity and not its own, the head-hunting entities forcibly removed Idulnas from Poha's body and abducted the demon to their own plane of existence.

The Bogeyman

CLASS VII. NONCORPOREAL.

For centuries, parents have used the threat of the bogeyman to frighten children into good behavior. Every culture has such lore, passed down across the generations, and there are many similarities between accounts of the creature: The bogeyman always comes at night, often has a sack in which to carry the worst of the children away, and can enter a bedroom through the closet or from under the bed.

In Europe and parts of Russia, folklore claims that the first true bogeyman was a monk, driven insane by the bad behavior of the local village children. He was so intent on correcting this that he made a deal with the devil: In exchange for his soul—and the regular sacrifice of the naughtiest of children—this monk, Rodefhiri (an anagram of the word "horrified") was given a cloak of invisibility and transformative features; he would appear to children as whatever frightened them most.

The Ghostbusters encountered Rodefhiri when he appeared in New York, manifesting atop One Times Square during New Year's Eve festivities. His intention was to spread fear amongst the crowd and feed on it—fear being the source of this bogeyman's power. With so many revelers gathered in Times Square, Rodefhiri became so powerful that we needed to use more than one trap to capture him.

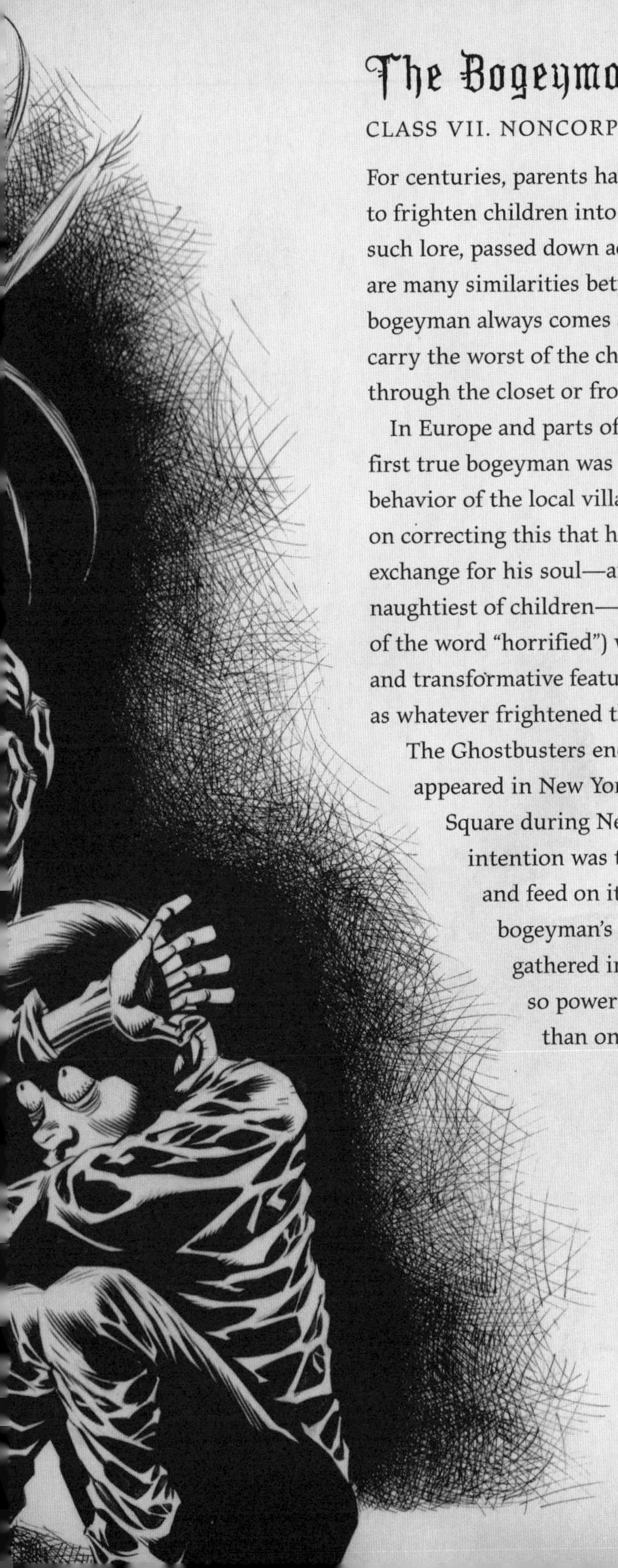

The Hungry Manitou

CLASS V. ANCHORED TO THE STATE OF NEW YORK. POSSESSOR. POWERFULLY MANIPULATIVE. CAN CONJURE ELABORATE PSYCHOKINETIC CONSTRUCTS.

The Hungry Manitou was a demon summoned by an Algonquian man to prey upon a small group of English settlers. The Manitou was highly effective in its slaughter—too effective, it transpired.

It killed those that it was sent after, but did not stop with them. The Manitou killed whole settlements—regardless of whether they were English or Algonquian. The death toll was so high that the Native American who had conjured the spirit regretted his actions and sought a way to banish the Hungry Manitou back to the spirit world.

He failed, but by using witchcraft, he was able to bluff his way into a deal with the demon; the Hungry Manitou would agree to sleep for decades at a time, allowing men to thrive, before he woke once again to feed on a limited number of victims and then returned to hibernation. This bloody cycle would continue throughout the years.

During the Hungry Manitou's most recent manifestation, the Ghostbusters were called in to deal with it at a theme park in Schenectady, New York. The entity had captured a group of park attendees, which made the situation extremely complicated and perilous.

The Manitou is a possessing entity that consumes its victims from the inside out, and was terrorizing people at the park with spectral constructs, including semi-autonomous demonic clowns, ghostly bats, and phantom monkeys. The Manitou was also able to animate objects from the park, at one point causing a number of carousel horses to break free and stampede.

During the course of our encounter, the Manitou took possession of our associate Dr. Venkman. Communicating with the Manitou on a psychic plane, Dr. Venkman put his psychology doctorate to full use and managed to exorcise the Manitou from his own body (a feat Dr. Spengler and I would like to attempt ourselves at some point, should a controlled experiment ever prove possible).

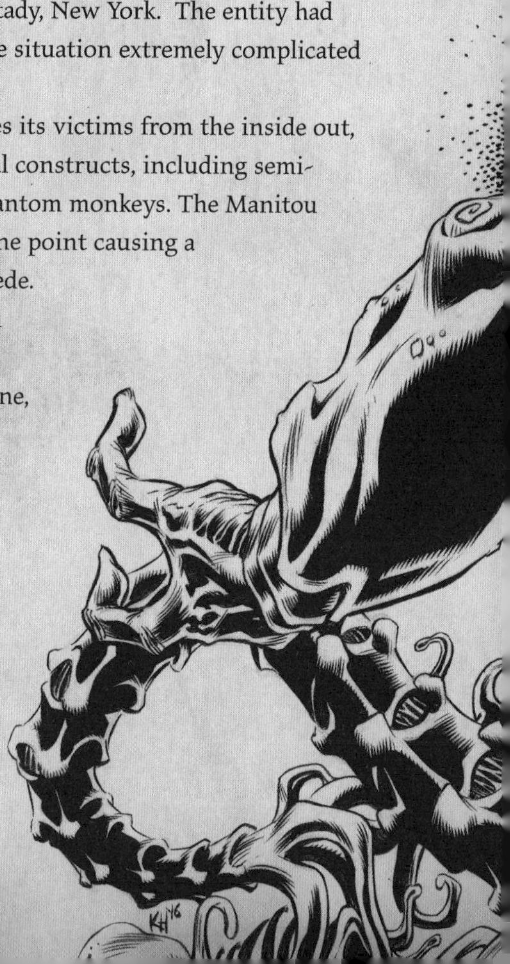

Once separated from its human host, the Manitou was no longer able to manipulate its environment psychokinetically or form any further spectral constructs. Our colleague Winston Zeddemore had set the Manitou's captives free while Dr. Venkman was possessed, leaving the entity with no other victims to possess. At this point, we were more easily able to contain and capture the threat.

The Boogaloo

CLASS VII. CORPOREAL.

POWERFUL, BUT BOUND BY A DEAL STRUCK WITH HUMANITY.

In ancient times, the British Isles were host to a particularly large group of demons that threatened to drive mankind away from the land. The entities also had the potential to spread to Europe and beyond, and the Druids, aware of the catastrophic potential that the creatures represented, moved to contain them.

They performed a difficult series of rituals and incantations in order to gain an audience with the demons' chieftain, sacrificing many of their number to ultimately subjugate the head demon with a spell.

Aware that if they killed the head demon, another would rise, they instead struck a deal with it: The creature would leave Earth for the void of limbo, taking its followers with it, but only if the Druids would agree to keep the memory of the demons alive. If mankind forgot about them completely, they would be allowed to return and overrun the world. The deal was struck.

The Druids were forced to adopt an oral history from that point on, as any attempt to write down the true name of the demon they had made the deal with led their writing implements to mysteriously burst into flames. As a result, the Druids dubbed this head demon the Boogaloo—a silly name to be sure, but one innocuous enough to avoid this spontaneous combustion.

In later years, many of the traditions of Halloween evolved as a way of keeping the memory of the demons alive and humanity safe from their malevolence.

More recently, however, Pleasant Valley, a small town in Dutchess County, New York, provided a loophole to the centuries-old deal, which the Boogaloo and its followers were able to exploit. The town had placed a ban on all Halloween activities, and so the Boogaloo and its minions were able to materialize there and wreak havoc. These demons were powerful enough that they were initially able to shrug off our proton streams completely.

The turning point came when they left the town limits and found the loophole closed: Halloween decorations were in full effect in nearby Poughkeepsie, proving that mankind had in fact kept up their end of the bargain. The Boogaloo and its followers willingly returned to exile.

Grundel

CLASS III. FULLY CORPOREAL PARASITIC BEING.

Few things are more horrifying than a Grundel. A parasitic entity not unlike the traditional vampire, the Grundel exists only to create more of its own kind.

Chillingly, these creatures prey only on children, seeking them out and isolating them before tempting them to commit sinful acts—theft, gluttony, and violence are most common. The creature cannot form a parasitic bond with a child without explicit permission from its intended victim, and these acts of malevolence are part of the Grundel's scheme to ingratiate itself with its victim. Having won the child's confidence, the Grundel feeds on its victim's soul, replacing it with its own foul essence. Eventually, the child's life is forfeit, it rises as a new Grundel, and the cycle repeats.

Grundels are mostly corporeal but can become intangible at will in dark spaces. The creatures are extremely photosensitive, and exposure to bright light can severely weaken them. They are of above average intelligence and will use any means necessary to achieve their goals. Consider them extremely dangerous.

The Ghostbusters have faced a Grundel on more than one occasion. When parasitically linked to a child, they can't be trapped; when that link is severed, they're no more of a challenge to trap than any other average class III entity. We have found that the most efficient way to separate a Grundel (or any possessing entity) from its host is to douse the host with positively charged psychomagnotheric slime.

Killerwatt

CLASS VII. ELEMENTAL ENTITY COMPOSED OF ELECTRICITY AND PSYCHOKINETIC ENERGY.

The Killerwatt entity (as nicknamed by Dr. Venkman) is a highly evolved elemental entity. It can manipulate electricity and possess virtually any object that runs on an electrical charge. It is also able to create subservient clones of itself, with similar—yet less powerful—abilities.

The Ghostbusters went head-to-head with the Killerwatt when it caused a series of power blackouts throughout New York City. In order to trap the entity, we had to disrupt the power for Manhattan, Queens, and a large portion of Brooklyn.* Once Killerwatt was disengaged from a direct flow of current, his minion-clones vanished, and we were able to trap him without further incident.

* This entry should in no way constitute a legal admission of any kind.
—LOUIS TULLY,
Ghostbusters legal counsel

Kestrel

CLASS IV. POSSESSOR.

EXTREMELY POWERFUL WHEN IN POSSESSION OF A HOST BODY.

The witch known as Kestrel was burned at the stake during the Salem witch trials of the 1690s. Unlike many of those who were executed during this time, Kestrel was actually guilty of the crime she was charged with. Before she was put to death, she threatened to enact revenge from beyond the grave.

Over three centuries later, Morgan Hrom, an opportunistic medium with her own TV show, heard about Kestrel and came to Salem to hold a séance as a publicity stunt. The séance was wildly successful, fully drawing Kestrel's spirit back to Earth.

Kestrel possessed Hrom's body and physically transmogrified it to match the witch's original human appearance. Kestrel told the crowds that had gathered to watch the show that her revenge was nigh and then began to attack the town, setting buildings on fire with her psychokinetic powers.

Kestrel proved extremely resistant to our usual method of counteracting a possessing entity (i.e., physical application of positively charged psychomagnotheric ectoplasm to the host body).

In the end, we had to modify one of our ghost traps on the fly in order to force Kestrel out of its host body long enough to snag it with a proton stream. Before being sucked into our trap, the entity conjured one final fire, engulfing the nearby Salem Witch Museum. The fire burned for three days, but the building still stands, unharmed. We've been itching to investigate this anomaly further. . . .

Lilith

CLASS VII. CORPOREAL. AFFINITY WITH ELECTRICITY. PARASITIC.

Cultures dating back to the Sumerians have told tales about Lilith, a demon said to feed on living organisms, including human beings. The stories state that Lilith consumed either the blood or the soul of its victims, however, our encounters with this entity have proved that it consumes neither. In fact, Lilith's primary food source is electricity.

In the days before modern technology provided such easy access to electricity, humans and other animals that produce bioelectricity would have been the sole source of sustenance for Lilith. As civilization became more advanced and the availability of domestic electricity increased, fatal attacks attributed to Lilith decreased—although they didn't stop entirely.

Our first Lilith-related call was at the East River Generating Station; unlike our experiences with the Killerwatt entity (see the entry on Killerwatt on page 56), we discovered that disconnecting the flow of power at the station didn't make this entity easier to trap. In fact, it only caused the still-hungry Lilith to attack bystanders until driven off by a boson dart—a burst of boson particles delivered from our proton packs that hits spectral targets like a grenade.

We went to plan B and lured Lilith to the firehouse by emitting a frequency matched to her own psychokinetic energy (P.K.E.) signature. Once she was there, the massive electrical output of the generators powering our ecto-containment unit was too much to resist. While she fed, we were able to trap her without further incident.

KH'16

Section IV: Gods and Major Demons

THE WORLD ENDERS, THE CONQUERORS,
AND OTHER CLASS VII THREATS TO HUMANITY

This section contains basic information on the worst of the worst: some of the more powerful entities that we've faced (with the exception Gozer and his connected entities, which are so despicable they deserve a dedicated section of their own). These entities present a threat to the world at large when they manifest. They see humanity as, at best, something to subjugate and, more often, something to destroy.

Prince Vigo of Carpathia

CLASS IV. POSSESSOR.

POWER ELEVATED BY PSYCHOMAGNOTHERIC ECTOPLASM.

Purported to be both alchemist and warlock, Prince Vigo of Carpathia was a cruel tyrant who came to prominence in the fifteenth century, ruling over his homeland and the conquered country of Moldavia.

After decades of his rule, his subjects rebelled and killed him; he was poisoned, shot, stabbed, hanged, and drawn and quartered—and still he clung stubbornly to life. He was 105 years old at the time of the coup, and yet, one of the Moldavians who rose against him later wrote that "he was as strong as any man in the prime of life."

Vigo hung on for days after the attack before perishing. His last words were, "Death is but a door, time is but a window. I'll be back!" He was finally beheaded and cremated, with his ashes scattered in the Black Sea. For years afterward, his subjects feared he was still watching them from beyond the grave.

Our encounter with Vigo coincided with the discovery of psychomagnotheric ectoplasm, also known as "mood slime." This psychokinetic substance has the ability to absorb and amplify both positive and negative emotions.

A veritable river of the stuff had built up over the years in one of New York's many abandoned subway tunnels, a byproduct of the high amount of spectral energy ever present in the metropolitan area. (It is our supposition that only the positivity brought in through the tourist trade and professional sporting victories has kept Manhattan from being consumed and destroyed in a flood of burning ectoplasm.)

Vigo's spirit lay dormant for centuries in an imposing portrait kept at the Manhattan Museum of Art. Using the weak-willed head of restorations, Dr. Janosz Poha, as his puppet, Vigo prepared for his return to the physical realm, feeding off the negative emotions stored in the mood slime to augment his own power.

Vigo's initial plan was to inhabit the physical form of museum employee Dana Barrett's infant son, Oscar. The Ghostbusters were able to prevent this from happening, but a furious Vigo, desperate for a host body, instead took possession of Dr. Stantz.

This was the first time we used positively charged mood slime to exorcise a possessed individual, and with Vigo drawing so much power from the mood slime's negatively charged counterpart, the results were explosive—Dr. Stantz was knocked back, leaving Vigo's presence hovering in front of the painting it had formerly inhabited. We continued to hose Vigo's ghost down with mood slime while corralling it with proton streams. This resulted in the entity being banished back into the painting, effectively eliminating his power, if not his consciousness. Had Vigo gained a stronger foothold into physical form, it is very likely that he would have had the potential to conquer the world.

Wat

CLASS VII. POSSESSOR.

Unlike many of its fellow demons, Wat is very patient and willing to observe and gather information for long periods of time before finally taking action. For example, Wat possessed a young California woman, Sarah Westlake, for the better part of the 1970s before being discovered and forcibly exorcised.

Wat is a dominating force of the underworld, a being for whom conquest is the only worthy pursuit. Its modus operandi is to use a host body to covertly bring about a world susceptible to its rule, if not going so far as to trigger biblical Armageddon.

In its most recent manifestation, consistent with previous accounts, Wat again took a subtle approach, disguising itself as a frail old woman and hiring the Ghostbusters to investigate what we were told was a haunted house. When we arrived, Wat, in its elderly lady guise, feigned shock and asked for sanctuary at our headquarters while we tackled the haunting.

It was an elaborate ruse; the demon had intended to release the contents of our ecto-containment unit and enlist the escaping ghosts into an army that could conquer mankind. Fortunately, increased security features on the containment unit prevented this.

Frustrated, Wat reverted to its true form and attacked us directly, causing minor cosmetic damage to the main floor of our headquarters before being overwhelmed and entrapped.

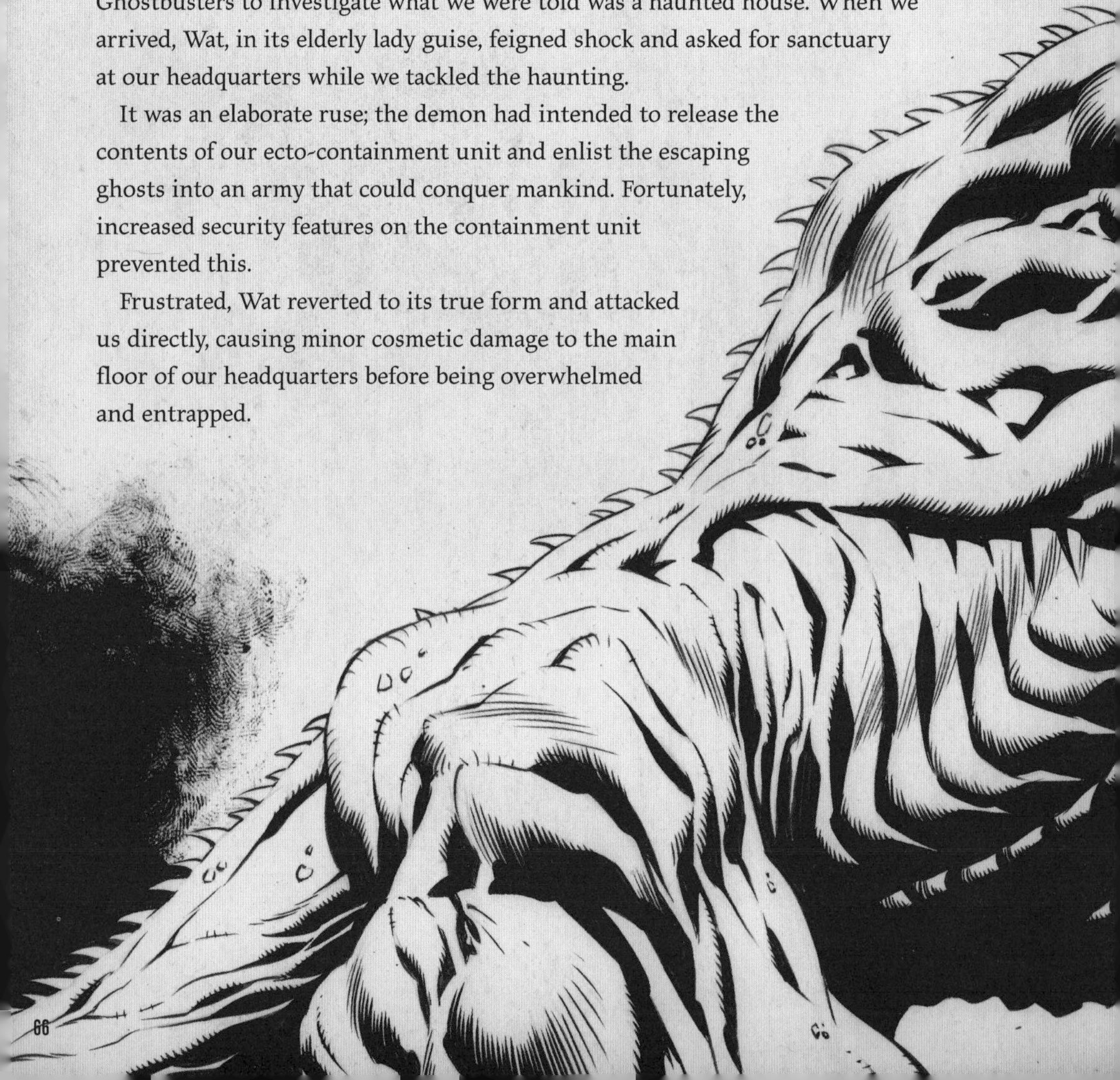

Samhain

CLASS VII. ABILITY TO MANIPULATE LOCAL ENVIRONMENT; CAN CONTROL LESSER ENTITIES.

The Gaelic festival of Samhain, traditionally held on October 31, marks the coming of winter and the time of year when apparitions may most easily cross over to the living world.

The spirit-king Samhain's goal is to expand that particular window, allowing the ghostly subjects he draws strength from to increase their presence on the mortal plane. With his power expanded exponentially by an upsurge in spirits, Samhain would be able to usher in an eternal autumn, ending all life as we know it.

Samhain is not the true name of this being; it is an alias adopted in order to minimize vulnerability. Knowledge of true names gives a measure of power, and power is something Samhain is not eager to share.

Samhain is capable of minor environmental manipulation: It projects an autumnal aura, and in its presence, temperatures drop, and leaves turn brown and fall from trees. At the height of its power, Samhain was also able to turn day into night, projecting a darkness over the city not seen since the manifestation of Gozer.

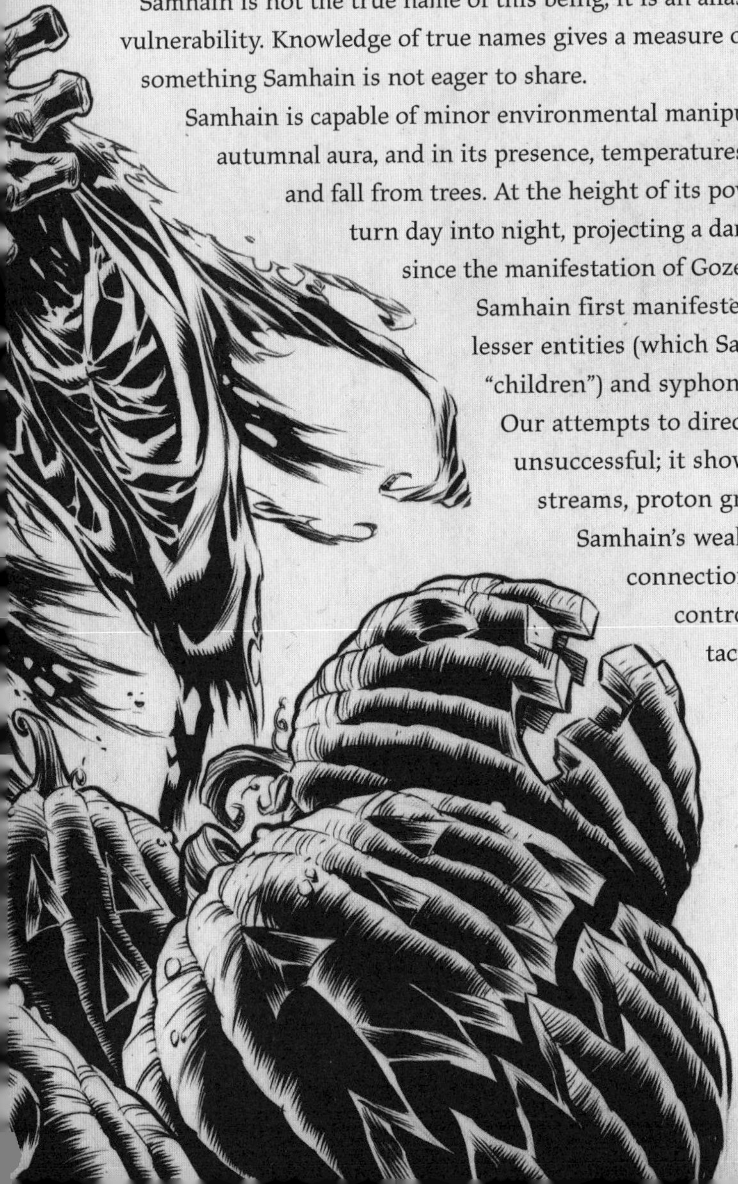

Samhain first manifested in Central Park, summoning lesser entities (which Samhain referred to as its "children") and syphoning strength from them.

Our attempts to directly attack Samhain were unsuccessful; it showed no reaction to proton streams, proton grenades, or boson darts.

Samhain's weakness came from its connection to the lesser entities it was controlling. When we changed tactics and began trapping those ghosts, Samhain became agitated—we were, essentially, removing its batteries. With the lesser entities trapped, Samhain was weakened to the point where we could facilitate its capture.

Cathulhu

UNCLASSIFIABLE.

At first glance, Cathulhu—with its many appearances in popular fiction—would seem an unlikely inclusion in this guide. However, we have discovered that the writers of stories that feature similar entities are often haunted by dreams with such specific continuity of detail that coincidence seems unlikely.

Cathulhu, for example, does exist and is a massively powerful entity—the act of trying to register its P.K.E. signature actually burnt out our reader.

There was initially no definitive proof of this being's existence aside from the susceptibility of several writers to Cathulhu's psychic influence. The entity was, in fact, reaching out to inspire the formation of a worshipful cult that would be able to summon its master to our plane of existence.

This Cult of Cathulhu very nearly succeeded; the bodies of the cult members were possessed and transmogrified into miniature versions of Cathulhu itself, and this infestation led to the involvement of the Ghostbusters.

The demigod itself manifested near Coney Island; it was slow-moving and enormous, much larger than the Stay Puft Marshmallow Man (see the entry on page 91). Cathulhu's presence also fouled the weather, causing a lightning storm to form despite the clear skies that had existed just moments before.

The initial application of four separate proton streams did not affect it; however, we successfully lured it to a roller coaster where we were able to attract lightning from the aforementioned storm by ionizing the track with our proton streams. This provided Cathulhu with a jolt in excess of 100 gigavolts; not enough to destroy it, but enough to convince it to return to a dormant state.

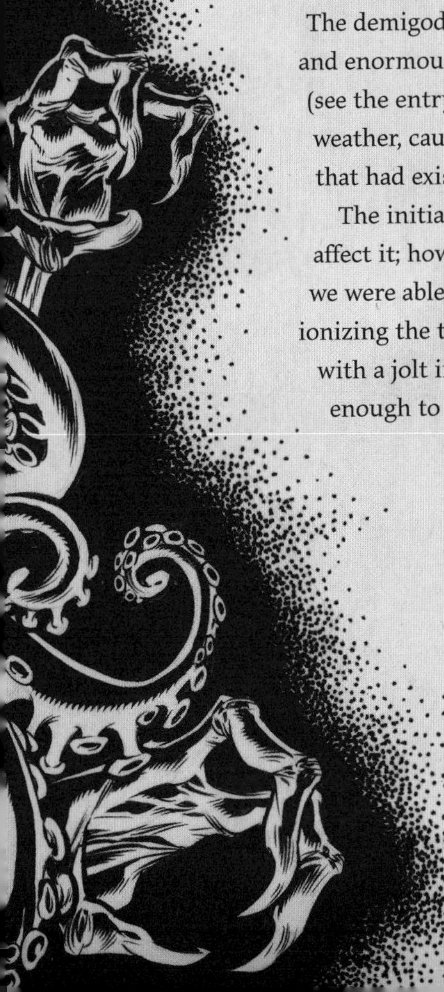

Hob Anagarak

CLASS VII. FIRE DEITY.

The lore of an obscure tribe of the Inuit people states that the Ice Age was caused when the fire god Hob Anagarak was defeated by his rivals, who imprisoned him within a chunk of obsidian.

Some members of the tribe that watches over the dormant Hob Anagarak prayed for his return—in their view, his connection to fire is holy and purifying, a power that will wipe away the evils of the earth. However, the majority of the tribe sees this fire god and his power as wholly destructive, something that will consume every living thing until nothing remains.

Our encounter with Hob Anagarak was purely a matter of research; we had heard about the obsidian prison and traveled north to inspect it. The stone that held the entity was located in a remote Alaskan village and was warm to the touch—despite being located above the Arctic Circle.

Its P.K.E. reading was well within range of a dormant entity, but in the interests of safety, we left behind a P.K.E. meter with remote transmission capability to give us some forewarning should the entity begin to stir.

Apshai

CLASS VI. INSECT DEMON.

Mentioned in an obscure essay by ancient Roman author Pliny the Elder, Apshai was described as a large, mantis-like demon who escaped the Egyptian underworld and returned to the land of the living, defying the sun god Ra.

Because of this defiance, Apshai avoided direct sunlight (to evade the gaze of Ra) and amassed its followers under cover of night. Ultimately, Apshai's goal was to turn the world into a lush green jungle and give it over to insects, its favored children.

When the cockroach population increased exponentially and began to cause disruption in the Bronx—at one point the insects were seen hauling off a hot dog cart—we were called in by City Hall to intervene. (We were brought in not because they thought it was a supernatural occurrence, but because they thought we could "atomize the bugs" with our proton packs.) The roaches, however, carried an abnormally high P.K.E. reading that caught our attention. Tracking the bugs to a point of convergence led us to an abandoned subway station and the newly manifested Apshai.

The clue we needed to defeat the demon came from the aforementioned works of Pliny the Elder. Through his writings we learned of Apshai's aversion to direct sunlight, which we exploited by destroying the ceiling of the subway station.* When the sunlight hit Apshai, its physical form combusted.

* With the cooperation of the NYPD, we would like to note.

—LOUIS TULLY, *Ghostbusters legal counsel*

Achira

CLASS VII. NONCORPOREAL POSSESSOR.

The demon Achira has been responsible for spreading untold disease and death throughout the world. It was the source of the infamous Black Death epidemic, numerous plagues from Russia to Milan, and, it's rumored, the Spanish influenza outbreak of the twentieth century.

In order to be effective, Achira must possess a willing and healthy host—if the host isn't strong enough, it will not long survive the strain of inhabitation. Curiously, the entity specifically seeks out individuals who desire revenge but feel powerless to take the necessary action. Playing on those feelings of impotence, Achira ingratiates its way into the victim's life before taking possession of their body.

When possessed, the host body takes on an increasingly horrific appearance, transmogrified into a form more pleasing to the entity. Exorcism is difficult in the case of Achira; the plague and pestilence it exudes is very real and threatens the life of any who intervene.

Our colleague Winston Zeddemore, a former Marine, was instrumental in our plan to trap this particular entity before it could unleash another pandemic. From a distance, Zeddemore accurately fired darts filled with concentrated antibiotics at Achira's host, driving the entity out and allowing us to trap it.

Lotan

CLASS VI. HARBINGER OF CATASTROPHIC DESTRUCTION.

Lotan is said to revel in creating devastation on a massive scale and manifests as a somewhat serpentine whale that swims through the sky. Sightings of the entity can be traced as far back as the time of Plato, who claimed that Lotan was present during the destruction of Atlantis.

Lotan was also seen by the survivors of Mount Vesuvius's eruption in AD 79, over London during the Blitz, and in the skies of Hiroshima before the atomic bomb was dropped.

Lotan manifested in New York during our encounter with Dumazu (see entry on facing page), circling the skies above the Museum of Natural History. As an entity that appears prior to massive destruction, Lotan, we believe, was drawn to the strong psychokinetic energy profile created by Dumazu's presence.

After the destruction of the Relic of Nilhe and Dumazu's subsequent retreat, Lotan, cheated of an anticipated catastrophe, began to go wild, bucking and swooping over the city. In its frenzy, it even knocked one of the eagles off the Chrysler Building.

Since our proton streams were ineffective against such a massive airborne entity, we needed an alternate method to subdue it. The armed forces assisted us in this matter with the loan of a UAV (unmanned aerial vehicle), which we rigged with proton explosives and remotely piloted right into Lotan's mouth.

The resulting proton explosion weakened the entity's molecular cohesion, causing it to disperse soon after. Though P.K.E. levels soon returned to normal, we still consider Lotan to be an active threat.

Dumazu

CLASS IV. LIVING GOD OF PRE-COLUMBIAN NORTH AMERICA.

Dumazu—not unlike the Carpathian Prince, Vigo—was a despotic ruler feared by his subjects. He was feared so much, in fact, that they worshipped him as their living god.

He lived for almost 130 years before finally passing on—or, as his followers called it, "ascending"—in 2010 BCE, with the promise to one day return to physical life and remake the world into a terrible paradise for his followers.

Dumazu was entombed in a cavern deep below what is now Manhattan and was largely forgotten by the world. In the late twentieth century, however, the spirit of the tyrant began to manifest in the dreams of his genetic descendants. These nocturnal visions featured a beast-faced demon that identified itself as Dumazu and demanded the "Relic of Nilhe."

The relic, a large, blue, crystal orb that was described in detail in these dreams, was later unearthed by one of these descendants during an excavation in Rhode Island. It was then put on display in the Museum of Natural History, where Dumazu's spirit attempted to claim it.

The entity managed a partial manifestation within the museum, transmogrifying several of the exhibits and forming them into a makeshift body. Application of positively charged psychomagnotheric slime had no effect on Dumazu's ersatz body. We were forced to fire upon the relic itself with a concentrated proton blast in order to prevent Dumazu from fully crossing over to this plane. The Relic of Nilhe was shattered but not destroyed. Before fully dispersing, Dumazu promised to return.

Section V: Gozer

THE TRAVELER AND THOSE WHO FOLLOW HIM

This section features information on the Sumerian god of destruction, Gozer the Gozerian, (aka Volguus Zildrohar, Lord of the Sebouillia, the Traveler, the Destructor) and those connected to him.

The modern-day arrival of this obscure deity, worshipped long ago by the Sumerians, Mesopotamians, and Hittites, was the closest the world has come to annihilation. Based on that fact alone, Gozer and his minions have earned a section of their own in this revised version of *Tobin's Spirit Guide*.

Gozer

CLASS VII. EXILED SUMERIAN DEITY OF DESTRUCTION.

The Sumerian deity Gozer, also worshiped by Mesopotamians and Hittites, was primarily associated with death and destruction and was believed to be the one that would bring about the world's eventual end. Gozer's followers were constantly trying to compel their god into triggering Armageddon.

A rival cult, which worshipped the chaos goddess Tiamat, Gozer's sibling, opposed the Gozerian goal of universal destruction. Encouraged by their deity, Tiamat's followers performed the rituals needed to banish Gozer from our plane of existence, forcing the Destructor to become a Traveler, wandering lost among the dimensions.

Though exiled from this plane, Gozer was not entirely forgotten—his followers dwindled in number over the millennia but never stopped trying to call their god back to Earth.

Gozer ultimately manifested at the site of a temple built atop 55 Central Park West, where he was confronted by the Ghostbusters. (The building was designed by cultist Ivo Shandor (see the entry on page 86) as a sort of spiritual radio tower created to better broadcast prayers to Gozer.) The Gozerian initially appeared as an androgynous humanoid with blood-red eyes and a new-wave haircut and demanded that we, as the race facing destruction, choose the form he would take to destroy our world. This opportunity to "choose the form of the destructor" is Gozer's one concession to those he annihilates.

Unfortunately for Gozer, the form chosen by a stray thought of Dr. Stantz's—that of the Stay Puft Marshmallow Man (see the entry on page 90)—was not nearly as formidable as other forms he had previously taken.

Ultimately, Gozer's physical essence was destroyed when we crossed our individual proton streams (risking total protonic reversal) and aimed them at the temple from which the deity had emerged into this plane of existence.

Later encounters revealed that although Gozer's physical essence was dispersed, his consciousness remained on Earth, attempting to find a new physical form and complete his mission of destruction.

Gozer has been successful at physical reconstitution on more than one occasion, but is now permanently locked into the form of the Stay Puft Marshmallow Man. The deity has tried to force a reselection in order to assume a more powerful form, but has been, as yet, unsuccessful.

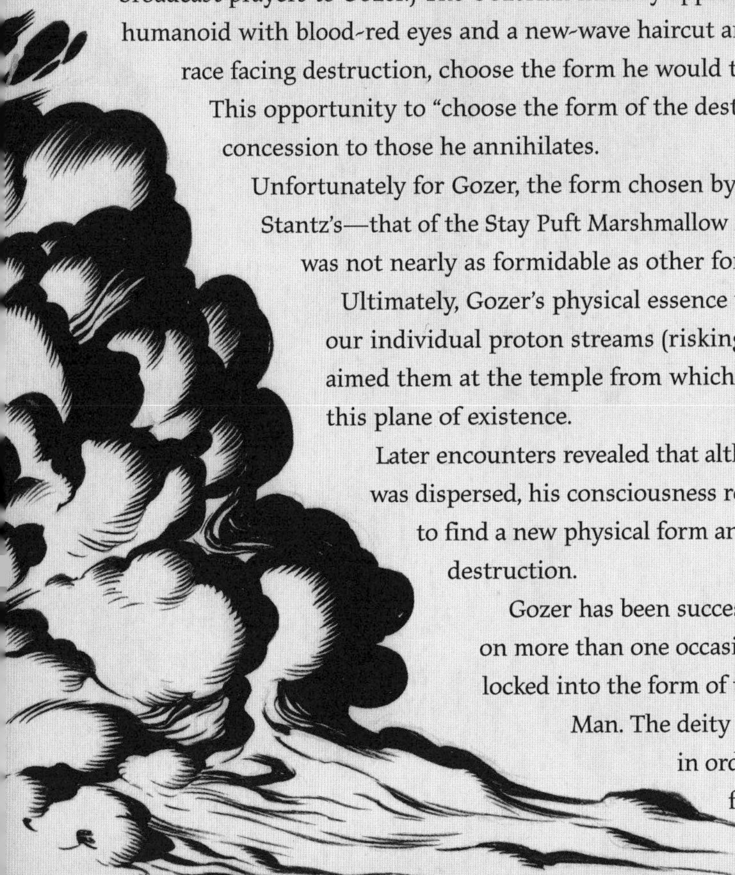

Vinz Clortho & Zuul

CLASS VII. FULLY CORPOREAL POSSESSORS.

For years, Gozerian cultists anticipated the coming of Vinz Clortho and Zuul, the minions and emissaries of Gozer, who would pave the way for the Destructor's coming—and the world's end.

The most powerful members of a race of other-dimensional, bearlike creatures that have sometimes been referred to as "terror dogs," Vinz Clortho and Zuul were possessing entities that could take over the bodies of any mortal species.

The two minions were able to travel inter-dimensionally in their search for beings they could use to bring about the coming of Gozer. Entering a new world, they would each find a mortal host and possess them; this would transform the hosts into the Keymaster and the Gatekeeper, the individuals who, once united, would perform the rites needed to summon Gozer.

Once the summoning was completed, the hosts would be transmogrified into Vinz Clortho and Zuul's true forms, demonic terror dogs. In our initial encounter with Gozer, Dana Barrett and Louis Tully played host to Gozer's emissaries, but when the deity was defeated, they were both returned to human form unharmed. (Although later tests showed that they retained mild aggressive tendencies and a taste for rare meat for several weeks afterward.)

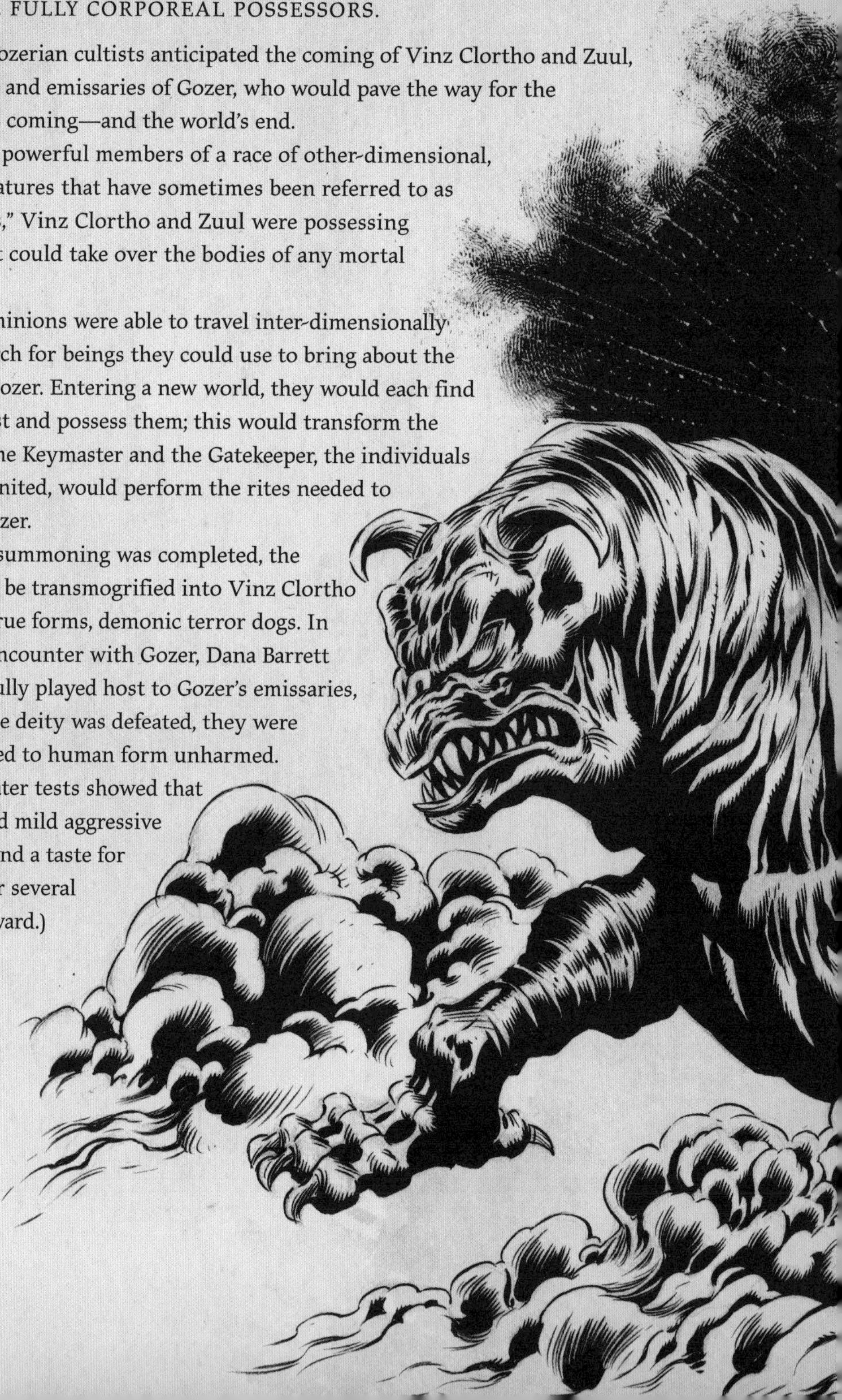

Idulnas

CLASS VII. POSSESSOR.

Idulnas, the third minion of Gozer, was a powerful entity. Like Vinz Clortho and Zuul, it was capable of possessing a being and transmogrifying this host body into a form that matched its own demonic appearance. It was also able to manifest through mirrors, panes of glass, and other reflective surfaces, and to use electrical energy as a weapon, much like its master, Gozer.

Idulnas was not one of the god's original servants; it was willed into existence by Gozer's residual essence in a last-ditch effort to force the selection of a new destructive form. (As previously mentioned, Gozer was trapped in the form of the Stay Puft Marshmallow Man (see the entry on page 90) following our initial encounter.) To achieve this end, Idulnas captured Dr. Stantz—who was responsible for initially selecting Gozer's Stay Puft form—and took him to the rebuilt Gozerian temple atop 55 Central Park West. Its attempts to pressure Dr. Stantz into selecting a new form for Gozer were thwarted by the arrival of the other Ghostbusters, however, and Idulnas was dispersed by the concentrated blast of a proton grenade.

Ivo Shandor

HUMAN SERVANT OF GOZER.

Born in Romania in or around 1855, Dr. Ivo Shandor was a man of many interests and talents, including mythology, science, and the arts.

Initially a surgeon, he was questioned more than once about his tendency to perform unnecessary operations on patients; there were also allegations of horrific experiments. One such story held that Shandor tried to give a living man a second heart to see if it improved bodily efficiency. Another rumor involved the attempted creation of a living centaur.

As noted, Shandor was a lover of mythology, and his readings eventually led him to become fascinated with the beliefs of the Cult of Gozer.

Though Shandor was never tried for any of the foul practices he was accused of, the rumors of his activities made it difficult for him to continue his deranged work. So he changed focus.

Moving to New York from Bucharest in 1898, Shandor turned to another love: architecture. He designed many buildings but ultimately only built one: the apartment tower at 55 Central Park West, upon which he erected a temple to Gozer.

Feeling that the human race didn't deserve to survive after the First World War, Shandor devoted the rest of his life to summoning an apocalypse at his rooftop temple, finally dying in 1934 from complications surrounding an experimental surgery he was performing on himself—reports say he was trying to carry out the first ever interspecies leg transplant.

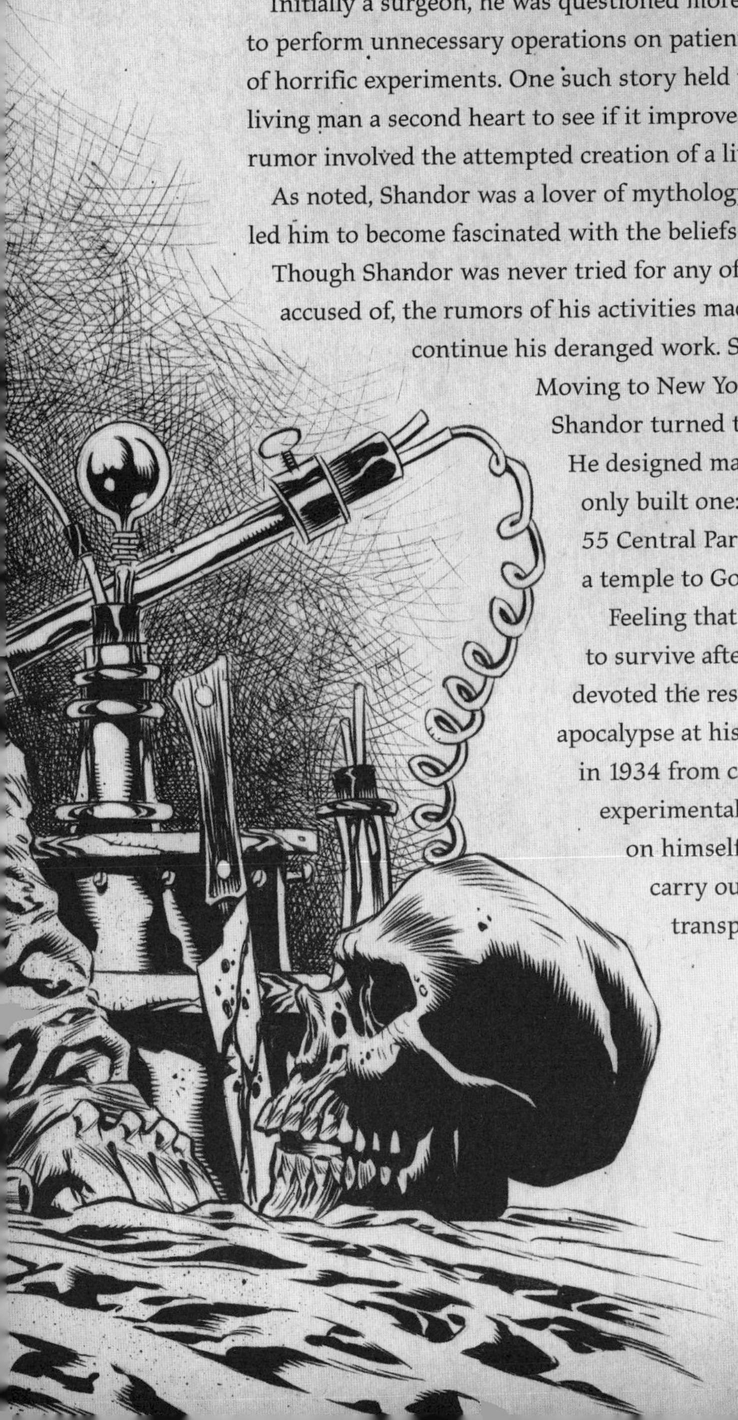

Tiamat

CLASS VII. SUMERIAN GODDESS; AN EMBODIMENT OF CHAOS.

A Sumerian chaos goddess, Tiamat cultivated an antagonistic rivalry with her brother Gozer, god of destruction, and this animosity filtered down to their respective cults, whose destructive clashes no doubt pleased both deities. Gozer's ultimate goal of ending existence as we know it clashed with Tiamat's love of the chaos inherent in life, and this conflict raged over many centuries.

According to the writings of the Gozerian Cult, circa 2800 BCE, it was Tiamat's followers—under her direct guidance—that were responsible for Gozer's banishment from this plane of existence. Roughly translated, the writings describe what sounds like a massive interdimensional crossrip at the time of Gozer's exile—the Gozerian temple in Shuruppak was said to burn for nine days under blood-red skies, while a host of misfortunes comparable to the biblical plagues of Egypt assaulted the populace.

With Gozer believed lost forever, the Gozerian Cult steadily lost both followers and influence to the many other gods of the Sumerian pantheon—primarily Tiamat.

Gozer's eventual return to this dimension in the twentieth century and his subsequent protonic disincorporation captured Tiamat's interest. These events brought her to New York to directly observe modern humanity and the Ghostbusters in particular. Her presence brought about a number of scientific anomalies (including blood raining from the sky, talking pigeons, and areas of unreliable gravity).

After a skirmish that led to the very edge of total protonic reversal, Tiamat left our plane of existence of her own volition, apparently pleased with the chaotic state of the world.

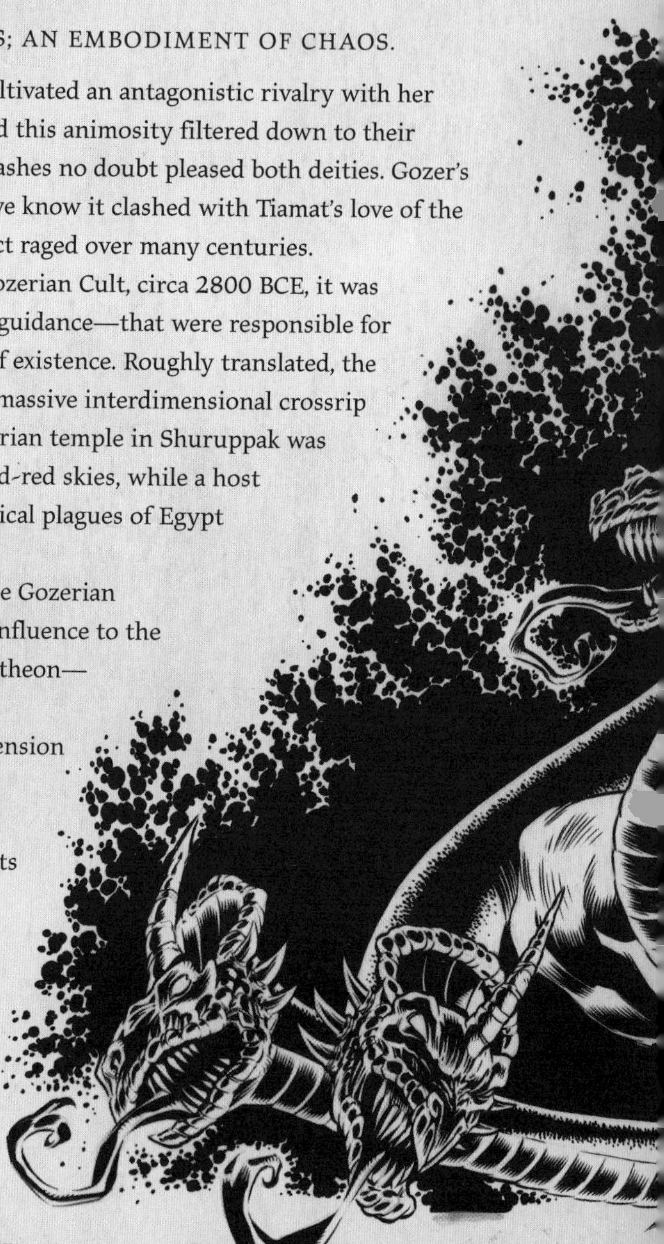

The Stay Puft Marshmallow Man

CLASS VII. GOZERIAN FORM.

As noted, Gozer allowed those he was about to destroy an opportunity to choose the form that this destruction would take; whatever form was chosen, no matter how bizarre, would appear and destroy the world. When Gozer manifested in New York, the Ghostbusters were tasked with making that choice.

Dr. Venkman recommended we clear our minds and not give an answer, but, as a god, Gozer was able to look into our minds anyway and pull from them the strongest image—in this case, Dr. Stantz's childhood memory of roasting Stay Puft marshmallows at Camp Waconda.

At the time, Dr. Stantz was trying to maintain a mental picture of innocence and think of things that couldn't possibly destroy the world; Gozer subverted this

intention and took the form of a hundred-foot-tall Stay Puft Marshmallow Man. Fortunately, the selection had its disadvantages: Stay Puft was slow-moving and had little offensive capability beyond its sheer size.

When we destroyed the temple Gozer had used as a gateway to this dimension, we also destroyed that particular manifestation of the Marshmallow Man; but this was not the last time Stay Puft appeared.

On several other occasions, psychokinetic energy has been abundant enough for Gozer to once again manifest as Stay Puft, but, with each successive manifestation, it has retained less potency, enabling us to deal with it in a relatively expedient manner (which is to say, we blew it up).

As noted in the Idulnas entry, there was an attempt to change Gozer's destructive form to something other than Stay Puft. When that failed, the Marshmallow Man manifested one final time. When we destroyed it, we used a modified trap to capture a significant portion of the Gozerian essence that drove it.

While we'd like to report that this means we've finally seen the last of the Stay Puft Marshmallow Man, any such certainty is virtually impossible when it comes to supernatural entities of this kind.

Other Chosen Forms of Gozer

The following information on Gozer's previous destructive forms is taken from an extended interview with Louis Tully (while possessed by the demonic presence known as Vinz Clortho, aka the Keymaster) and is presented for the sake of a more complete profile of Gozer.

Torb

During the rectification of the Vuldronaii,
the Traveler came as a large and moving torb.
—Vinz Clortho

Semiserpentine goliaths resembling eels with muscular arms, torbs emitted a continuous current, electrocuting any living creature that they did not crush or devour.

Sloar

During the Third Reconciliation of the last of the Meketrex Supplicants, they chose a new form for him—that of a giant sloar! Many shubs and zulls knew what it was to be roasted in the depths of a sloar that day, I can tell you.

—Vinz Clortho

The sloar is a large eyeless creature, a living furnace whose innards slowly burn that which it consumes. When Gozer took the form of a sloar, those it ate were burned while still alive.

Afterword

When Dr. Stantz first broached the subject of adapting and abridging *Tobin's Spirit Guide*, I admit that my initial response was hesitation; as Dr. Stantz noted in his introduction, selecting the content for an abridged version would (and did) take a significant amount of our downtime, which is in short supply as it is. I was also in the midst of a sensitive series of experiments involving the reaction of our stores of emotionally charged ectoplasm to various psychotropic pharmaceutical compounds and wasn't sure I could spare the time required to sift through such an enormous amount of information.

However, Dr. Stantz's enthusiasm for this adaptation was not dissimilar to that which drove our research into the paranormal and led to our work as Ghostbusters in the first place. Suffice it to say, considering that our work has prevented the end of the known world, I've learned there is value in trusting Dr. Stantz's instincts.

In reading this book, you'll have noticed information on common entities that you might come across in everyday life as well as the more extreme types that, with luck, you will not, such as demons, gods, or metaspecters.

However, please note that all supernatural entities should be handled with caution. For the Ghostbusters, direct interaction with powerful supernatural entities is often tenable only because of our specialized equipment. As such, you should avoid any such direct contact of your own, which could easily result in death, injury, or perhaps even being pulled into an adjacent dimension and tortured for eternity.

That said, it is still our hope that, through exposure to this work, some of you will be inspired to follow in our footsteps—and indeed, the footsteps of John Tobin—to shed light on the unknown through further research.

That would be good.

—Dr. Egon Spengler

New York, NY

INSIGHT
EDITIONS

PO Box 3088
San Rafael, CA 94912
www.insighteditions.com

Find us on Facebook: www.facebook.com/InsightEditions
Follow us on Twitter: @insighteditions

Published by Insight Editions, San Rafael, California, in 2016.

Library of Congress Cataloging-in-Publication Data available.

ISBN: 978-1-60887-708-9

Publisher: Raoul Goff
Acquisitions Manager: Robbie Schmidt
Art Director: Chrissy Kwasnik
Executive Editor: Vanessa Lopez
Senior Editor: Chris Prince
Production Editor: Elaine Ou
Editorial Assistant: Katie DeSandro
Production Manager: Thomas Chung

Illustrations by Kyle Hotz

Insight Editions would like to thank
Ivan Reitman, Eric Reich, and Virginia King.

ROOTS of PEACE REPLANTED PAPER

Insight Editions, in association with Roots of Peace, will plant two trees for each tree used in the manufacturing of this book. Roots of Peace is an internationally renowned humanitarian organization dedicated to eradicating land mines worldwide and converting war-torn lands into productive farms and wildlife habitats. Roots of Peace will plant two million fruit and nut trees in Afghanistan and provide farmers there with the skills and support necessary for sustainable land use.

Manufactured in China by Insight Editions

20 19 18 17 16 15 14 13 12